Tiny on the Farm

by Cari Meister

illustrated by Rich Davis

Viking

VIKING
Published by Penguin Group
Penguin Young Readers Group, 345 Hudson Street, New York, New York 10014, U.S.A.
Penguin Group (Canada), 90 Eglinton Avenue East, Suite 700, Toronto, Ontario, Canada M4P 2Y3
(a division of Pearson Penguin Canada Inc.)
Penguin Books Ltd, 80 Strand, London WC2R 0RL, England
Penguin Ireland, 25 St Stephen's Green, Dublin 2, Ireland (a division of Penguin Books Ltd)
Penguin Group (Australia), 250 Camberwell Road, Camberwell, Victoria 3124, Australia
(a division of Pearson Australia Group Pty Ltd)
Penguin Books India Pvt Ltd, 11 Community Centre, Panchsheel Park, New Delhi – 110 017, India
Penguin Group (NZ), 67 Apollo Drive, Rosedale, North Shore 0632, New Zealand
(a division of Pearson New Zealand Ltd.)
Penguin Books (South Africa) (Pty) Ltd, 24 Sturdee Avenue, Rosebank, Johannesburg 2196, South Africa

Penguin Books Ltd, Registered Offices: 80 Strand, London WC2R 0RL, England

First published in 2008 by Viking, a division of Penguin Young Readers Group

10   9   8   7   6   5   4   3   2   1

LIBRARY OF CONGRESS CATALOGING-IN-PUBLICATION DATA
Meister, Cari.
Tiny on the farm / by Cari Meister ; illustrated by Rich Davis.
p. cm.
Summary: Eliot and his big dog, Tiny, visit a farm and help Eliot's uncle find
a missing litter of kittens.
ISBN 978-0-670-06246-1 (hardcover)
[1. Farm life—Fiction. 2. Dogs—Fiction. 3. Cats—Fiction. 4. Animals—Infancy—Fiction.]
I. Davis, Rich, date– ill. II. Title.
PZ7.M515916Tgo 2008
[E]—dc22
2007023121

Manufactured in China
Set in Journal Text
Book design by Kate Renner

For Grandma and Grandpa
on the farm
—C. M.

To Daniel and David
You're the best! I love you.
—Dad

This is my dog, Tiny.

He's the best dog in the
whole world . . . and the biggest!

Everybody loves Tiny.
Especially Uncle John.
"Watch this, Uncle John!
Sit, Tiny! Good dog!

"Watch this, Uncle John!
Shake, Tiny! Good dog!

Uncle John's cat had kittens, but no one can find them. I'm sure Tiny can. After all, he has a great big nose!

"Come on, Tiny!

First we look in the milk house.
I find a pail. Tiny finds a
grasshopper. But no kitties.

In the hayloft, I find a tennis ball. Tiny finds an old barn boot. But no kitties.

In a horse stall, I find a brush. Tiny finds a horseshoe. But no kitties.

In the chicken coop,
I find a fluffy baby chick.
Tiny finds a rooster.
Watch out, Tiny!

In the shed, I don't see
anything but some old tires.
"There's nothing here, Tiny.
Where could those kitties be?"

But Tiny won't leave the shed.

WOOF! WOOF! WOOF!
"What did you find, Tiny?"
Look! Tiny found the kitties!
Good dog, Tiny!

The kitties are so cute! Some of them have stripes like their mama. Some of them are black. There are two that look almost the same. Watch out, Tiny!

The twin black kitties love Tiny a lot.
"It looks like Tiny has made some new
friends," says Uncle John.

Soon it is time to go home.
"Thanks for finding the kitties," says Uncle John.

"You and Tiny are the best cat detectives of all time."

the end!